THIS BOOK
BELONGS TO

_____

(who loves ketchup too)

For Millie, Oliver and Ruby
(the original ketchup-eating monsters)
and in loving memory of Nicola and Ruby
who are missed everyday.
We hope heaven has ketchup too.

First published in Great Britain in 2015
by Fourth Wall Publishing
2 Riverview Business Park, Shore Wood Road,
Bromborough, Wirral CH62 3RQ

Copyright © Adam Bestwick 2015

ISBN: 978-1-910851-86-9

Printed in the China.

fourth wall
publishing

more ketchup please!

written
and illustrated by
Adam Bestwick

Ruby

Take note of this true story,
(it's not made-up of course)
About my sister Ruby
and her love for tomato sauce.
So if you do know someone,
who is a ketchup fan,
Please make sure you tell them
how our problems all began. . .

When Ruby was a baby,
Dad made a
big mistake →
He fed her the wrong bottle
when he wasn't quite awake!

From that day on it all went wrong
and nothing passed her lip,
...without a generous
topping of...
Ruby's favorite dip!

She splodged ketchup on her baby food
and ketchup on her toast...

Ketchup on her buttered bread
and on her porridge oats!..

But when the bottle emptied,
and no more could be squeezed...
Ruby screamed and yelled out loud—

I WANT
MORE KETCHUP
PLEASE!

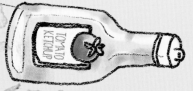

As Ruby started growing up,
one bottle didn't last,
Our little local corner shop
was running out too fast!

Dad went to supermarkets
and emptied all their shelves,
And staff were filling carts
like busy little elves!

Meanwhile at home...

She glugged ketchup on her boiled egg (and even in her soup)...

ketchup on her ice cream too...

that poured out with a

gloop!

But when the bottle emptied,
and no more could be squeezed...
Ruby screamed
and screamed again...

"**I WANT MORE KETCHUP** PLEASE!"

Oh no... she's going to... scream!

To keep our Ruby quiet, and avoid her piercing shriek,
My Dad would shop for ketchup maybe 18 times a week!..

I suggested to my mom..."let's make ketchup of our own,"
so we made our back garden a tomato-growing zone!

While they grew...

She covered pizza and potatoes...
(she liked it more
than mustard)

...and tomato sauce on
ALL desserts
(which dripped into the custard!)

But when the bottle emptied,
and no more could be squeezed...
Ruby screamed
with bright red cheeks...

Dad sprayed tomatoes
day and night,
to make them grow more quickly.
While Ruby kept on eating sauce,
It didn't make her sickly!

Next morning...
The neighbors weren't too happy
when we stopped going to the store,
We blocked our street with rows of trucks
bringing ketchup to our door!

As they delivered...

Ruby glopped ketchup on her doughnuts, (and smeared it 'round her lips!)...

Ketchup on her Brussels sprouts...

...and loads more on her chips!

But when the bottle emptied,
and no more could be squeezed...
Ruby screamed **"THERE'S NO MORE SAUCE!.."**

"I WANT MORE KETCHUP PLEASE!"

Ruby's news went 'round the world as supplies were running low...

While we squished our own tomatoes just as fast as they could grow!..

Mom called on all the countries,
from Japan to the United States...
"Send every ketchup bottle
that you have in wooden crates!"

While Mom phoned...

She covered cookies and sweet waffles in a thick, red, gloopy lake...

...and Ruby even splodged it all over chocolate cake!..

But when the bottle emptied,
and no more could be squeezed...
Ruby screamed,

"WE'RE
RUNNING OUT!"

"I WANT
MORE
KETCHUP,
PLEASE!"

As helicopters flew over, to drop off their supply,
The Army and the Navy were all waiting on stand-by...

Ruby dipped her fries in sauce
and had a juicy suck,
But to our surprise,
she quickly stopped...
and let out a big

yUck!

Then Ruby said...

"I don't like ketchup anymore - I'm finished with red dip...

...with creamy Mayonnaise!